Missing Ummi

Story by Jill Bryant
Illustrations by Martín Bustamante

Contents

Chapter 1

Goodbye, Ummi

Author's note:

Ummi (say: *oo-mi*) is Arabic for 'mother' or 'mum'.

Maya and her mum were walking home
from school together on Friday afternoon.
"Are we going to the park this weekend, Ummi?"
asked Maya.

Ummi stopped.
"Not this weekend, Maya. I have some news," she said.
"On Sunday, I have to go overseas for work.
I'm going to Germany. I'll be gone for a week.
My good friend Willow will come and take care of you."

Maya felt worried. She had never been apart from Ummi for a whole week before. "A week is a long time, Ummi!" she said.

"I must go, Maya," said Ummi. "But you will have fun with Willow."

Willow arrived on Sunday afternoon.

Maya watched as her mum finished packing her bags. Soon, it was time for Ummi to go.

"Goodbye, Maya," said Ummi.

"Goodbye, Ummi!" said Maya, sadly.

She and Willow watched as Ummi got into a taxi. *I wish Ummi didn't have to go away*, thought Maya.

Chapter 2

Maya and Willow

"I'm missing Ummi," Maya said to Willow, later that night.

"Sometimes when I feel sad, I like to draw," said Willow. She reached into her bag and handed Maya a tin of beautiful pencils.
"Why don't you draw a picture for your mum?" she asked.

"That's a good idea," said Maya.

Maya got some paper and began to draw.
She drew Ummi's plane.
It was speeding across a night sky.

"I think I'll draw a new picture for Ummi every night," she said.

Before school on Monday morning, Maya said to Willow, "I wonder where Ummi is now."

"Let's find out," said Willow.

She opened an app on her phone.
On the screen was a map.
Willow put in a number at the top of the screen.
A little plane appeared on the map.

"She's there," said Willow, pointing at the plane.

“The plane is over Germany,” said Maya.
“That must mean Ummi will land soon!”

At school on Wednesday, Maya found a note in her lunch bag.

After school, Willow made a video call to Ummi on her laptop.
Ummi's face appeared.

"Hello, Ummi!" said Maya.

"Hello, Maya!" said Ummi.

Maya told Ummi what she had done at school that day.
And she told her about finding the plane on Willow's phone.

Later that night, before bed, Maya said, "It was so good to talk to Ummi today. Thank you."

Willow smiled.

Chapter 3

Welcome Home!

On Saturday, Maya said,
"Ummi will be home tomorrow, Willow.
Can I show you all my pictures?"

"Yes," said Willow.

Willow looked at the pictures.
"They are very good," she said.
"Why don't you put them all in a special box?
I have one that I think is just right."

Maya carefully rolled up the pictures
and put them into the box.
Then, she gave Willow a hug.
"Thanks for taking care of me," Maya said.

On Sunday, Maya waited for the sound of her mum's taxi.
Suddenly, she heard a car door slam.
"Willow, it's Ummi!" said Maya.

The front door opened.
Maya jumped up and gave her mum a big hug.

Then, she gave Ummi the special box.

Ummi unrolled the pictures.
"Wow!" she said. "I love them."

"The pictures were Willow's idea," said Maya.

Maya turned to Willow.

"Willow, if Ummi has to go away again, can you please look after me?"

"Yes!" said Willow, with a smile. "Next time, I'll bring my paints with me."